Tuscanini

by Jim Propp

illustrated by Ellen Weiss

Bradbury Press • New York

Maxwell Macmillan Canada   Toronto
Maxwell Macmillan International
New York   Oxford   Singapore   Sydney

For Sandy
&
with thanks to Theresa
—*J. P.*

For Mollie
—*E. W.*

Bradbury Press
Macmillan Publishing Company
866 Third Avenue
New York, NY 10022

Maxwell Macmillan Canada, Inc.
1200 Eglinton Avenue East
Suite 200
Don Mills, Ontario M3C 3N1

Macmillan Publishing Company is part of the
Maxwell Communication Group of Companies.

First American edition
Printed and bound in Hong Kong by South China
Printing Company (1988) Ltd.
10 9 8 7 6 5 4 3 2 1

The text of this book is set in 16 point Caslon Book.
The illustrations are rendered in pen-and-ink and watercolor.
Typography by Julie Y. Quan

LIBRARY OF CONGRESS CATALOGING-IN-PUBLICATION DATA
Propp, Jim.
Tuscanini / by Jim Propp ; illustrated by Ellen Weiss. — 1st American ed.
p.   cm.
Summary: A music-loving elephant realizes his dream of becoming a
conductor after foiling a robbery attempt at the zoo.
ISBN 0-02-774911-8
[1. Elephants—Fiction.   2. Zoos—Fiction.   3. Musicians—
Fiction.]   I. Weiss, Ellen, ill.   II. Title.
PZ7.P9434Tu   1992
[E]—dc20   91-240

Once upon a hill in the middle of a zoo
lived an elephant named Tuscanini.

Every morning the zookeeper would visit him and bring him fresh hay and water to keep him well fed and cool.

Tuscanini would try to share the hay
with his friend the zookeeper. But
the keeper never wanted to eat any.

Tuscanini also tried to share
his water with the zookeeper.
The zookeeper liked that even less.

But the best thing that the zookeeper brought
with him was something they both could share:
MUSIC.

Tuscanini loved the music, and while he
listened to it he would happily wave his trunk
around, conducting an imaginary orchestra
that only he could see.

Sometimes the zookeeper would
sing along in a big tenor voice,
and Tuscanini would be very happy.

One summer day two pandas were brought
to the zoo. There was a big celebration
in their honor, because pandas are a dwindling species
and need encouragement.

Many famous and important people were there.

One elegant lady in a long dress
looked very hot and uncomfortable.
Tuscanini felt sorry for her and thought
he would do her a favor. He filled
his trunk with water and sprayed a
gallon of it right at her.

"Eek!" shrieked the lady. It was the highest, most piercing shriek Tuscanini had ever heard. The lady did not look happy.

The zookeeper was not happy either.
"That was Madame LaScala, the great opera singer.
You have made her upset."
Now Tuscanini was unhappy, too.
"Tell her I'm sorry," he said. "I only meant
to help her cool off." But it was too late
to apologize; the opera-lady had gone away,
wet and angry.

Tuscanini felt so bad about what he had done that he couldn't sleep that night. If only he hadn't sprayed water at Madame LaScala, maybe they would have been friends. She might even have sung an aria for him.

While Tuscanini was pacing on his hill in the middle of the zoo in the middle of the night, two men with flashlights climbed over the fence.

Tuscanini heard them talking as they crept around to where the pandas were.

"Why not ask the city for *two* million dollars?" said one of the men.

"One million for each of them! That's good." The other snickered as he unlatched the door of the pandas' cage.

Tuscanini knew what must be going on. These men had come to steal the pandas!

"Wake up!" brayed Tuscanini in his loudest voice.
"Wake up, everybody! There are kidnappers
in the zoo!" All the animals woke up and
made noise.

The two men became nervous.
"Let's grab the pandas and get out of here
before all this noise brings the police."
So they picked up the pandas and ran.

From high on his hill in the middle of the zoo,
Tuscanini could see the bad men running past the
monkey house. So he pointed his trunk at the monkeys.

All the other animals got quiet and the
monkeys went, "Hee, Hee, Hee!"—as if to say,
"*Here* they are!"

Then the men went running past the
tropical birds' cage. So Tuscanini wagged
his trunk at the birds. The monkeys became
quiet and the birds went, "Caw, Caw!"—as if
to say, "*Here* they are!"

The men took a sharp turn and started
running past the lion's lair. Tuscanini waved
his trunk at the lion.

The birds became quiet and the lion went,
"Roar!"—as if to say, "*Here* they are!"

"This is ridiculous!" said one of the
bad men. "The only way to escape from the zoo
is to stop that elephant."
"We'll tie its trunk in a knot," said the other.

The two men put the pandas down and
raced up the hill to where the elephant was.

When Tuscanini saw them coming toward him,
he filled his trunk with water, and when
they came close to him he shot the mightiest blast
he could, right at the two bad men.

POW! It knocked both of them to the ground.
In fact, it knocked them down so hard
they couldn't get up again.
    And that is where the police found them
a few minutes later.

The next day there was another big celebration,
this time in honor of Tuscanini.
Many famous and important people were there,
including Madame LaScala.

"Tuscanini is very sorry," the zookeeper told her.
"He meant well, and he says he will do you
any favor in the world if you forgive him."

"Of course I forgive you," said the opera-lady,
giving Tuscanini a friendly pat. "But there
is a favor you can do for me. The conductor
of the City Opera is sick.
Would you take his place tonight?"

That night, after Tuscanini had finished
conducting *Aida* at the City Opera, people in the
audience cried, "Bravo!" and "Magnificent!"

They threw him bouquets of flowers.

Then, from onstage, Madame LaScala tossed him
a bushel of hay. It was the nicest present
Tuscanini could imagine.